DO NOT REMOVE
CARDS FROM POCKET

About the Book

Poor Oscar Raccoon! Now that all the newspaper headlines are coming out wrong, bossy Theodore Cat, the newspaper's editor, may *never* find time to read Oscar's story.

Theodore is frantically busy trying to find out why SaDeeRoBanks and other puzzling headlines are being printed. He doesn't even know how to read them!

Could Humphrey Snake, Gertrude Flamingo, or the Jeremy P. Rat family have anything to do with this mystery? And will Theodore ever stop yowling and pacing long enough to read Oscar's story?

The antics of the *Claws 'n' Paws* newspaper staff are sure to delight beginning readers. They will enjoy figuring out how to read the misspelled headlines—with a little help from Oscar—in Malcolm Hall's imaginative, zany story, filled with comic characters and a marvelously detailed newspaper office drawn by the inimitable Wallace Tripp.

COWARD, McCANN & GEOGHEGAN, INC.   NEW YORK

HEADLINES

by Malcolm Hall

pictures by
   Wallace Tripp

About the Series

Boys and girls who are just beginning to read on their own will find the *Break-of-Day* books enjoyable and easy to read. Lively, fresh stories that are far-ranging and varied in content combine with attractive illustrations. Large, clear type and simple language, but without vocabulary controls, keep the stories readable and fun.

Text copyright © 1973 by Malcolm Hall
Illustrations copyright © 1973 by Wallace Tripp
All rights reserved. This book, or parts thereof, may not
be reproduced in any form without permission in writing from
the publishers. Published simultaneously in
Canada by Longman Canada Limited, Toronto.
SBN: GB-698-30482-9
SBN: TR-698-20230-9
Library of Congress Catalog Card Number: 72-85616
PRINTED IN THE UNITED STATES OF AMERICA
06209

To my grandmother,
Isabelle Hamilton

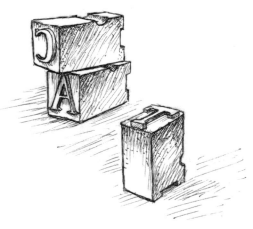

The animals were putting
the newspaper to bed.
"Putting a paper to bed"
doesn't mean tucking it in for
the night, of course.
It means getting ready
to print the paper.

They all worked together.

Frank Beaver

read each story aloud.

Caroline Porcupine took tiny

metal letters, called type,
out of a wooden box.
These letters
spelled out the stories.

Then the Jeremy P. Rat family
carried the type,
one letter at a time,
over to the printing press.

Morris Squirrel put the letters
on a wide tray.
There the type would be used
to print the paper.

Theodore Cat was
the editor of the paper.
It was his job to read the stories
and decide which ones to print.

Most of the time, however,
Theodore just sat at his desk
thinking about
what a great editor he was.
Oscar Raccoon, a reporter,
walked up to Theodore.
Oscar was mad!

He had written a story, but
Theodore wouldn't
put it in the paper.
"Why won't you print my story?"
asked Oscar.

Theodore put his paws
over his eyes.
The truth was that Theodore
hadn't even read Oscar's story.
But Theodore did not want
to admit it.

So he made up a reason.

"Your story was too long, Oscar."

"But my story was only
half a page long," said Oscar.

"Then it was too short,"
said Theodore.

And Theodore leaned back
in his chair and smiled
as only a cat can.

Just at that moment,
a great sound
of *whumpeta thumpeta*
filled the office.
Theodore jumped up, saying,
"I can't talk anymore, Oscar.
I've got to check the paper.
There's no telling what
might happen if I'm not there."

Theodore trotted
over to the printing press.
Wheels were turning;
ink was splashing;
paper was spinning around.
Hundreds of tiny letters

were printing the news.
Suddenly the printing press
shot out the first
copy of the newspaper.
Wham!
Right into Theodore's stomach.

Theodore got up slowly
and dusted himself off.
Then he picked up the paper
and started to read.
Then Theodore's face fell.

He began to pull his fur.
When he found his fur
was too short,
he pulled his whiskers instead.
"Stop the presses,"
yowled Theodore.

Everything came to a stop.
Frank began to bite at his nails.
Caroline started to knit.

The Jeremy P. Rat family ran
underneath the printing press
and peeped out nervously.
Theodore held up the paper.
"Who wrote this headline?"
he shouted.

Everyone stared.

The headline said:

SaDeeRoBanks

Gertrude Flamingo,

who wrote the society page,

began to flutter.

She stood on one leg

and flapped her wings.

"*I* didn't write it," she said.

"*I* can't even read it."

"I can't read it either,"

said Theodore.

"Can anyone read it?"

For a moment

no one spoke.

Then Humphrey Snake
began to clear his throat.
This took quite a while
because Humphrey had
quite a long throat.

Finally,

Humphrey was able to speak.

"It says, SADE EROB ANKS!"

All of the animals gasped.

Some even began

to clap their hands.

Theodore said, "Very good,
Humphrey,
but what does it mean?"
"How should I know?"
asked Humphrey.
"You only asked me
if I could read the headline.
You never asked me
if I knew what it meant.
The two aren't the same,
you know."
"They certainly are,"
yelled Theodore.
And for a moment
it looked as if

Humphrey and Theodore were
going to have a fight right there.

Suddenly Oscar spoke up.
"I can read it," he said, "and
I know what it means, too.
The headline says,
SAD DEER ROB BANKS."
Oscar had figured out
how to read the headline.

The last letter of one word
was also the first
letter of the next word.
Theodore puffed himself up.
"Whoever wrote that Sad Deer
story just lost his job.
No one can work for me
if he can't spell."

"But, Theodore," Frank said,
"you wrote that story yourself."
When Theodore heard this,
his eyes went wide open and
his whiskers rolled up like a rug.
Then Theodore became
very angry.
"Who did this to my story?"
he cried.

"This afternoon six deer
robbed five banks.
After a while, they felt so sorry
for the animals whose money
they had taken, they began to cry.
So my headline was
SAD DEER ROB BANKS.
We have to fix it!"

But there was nothing the animals
could do about the headline.
It was too late
to print the paper over again.

So the next day,
when the paper came out,
the headline still said:
SaDeeRoBanks.
At first, the animals who bought
the paper were puzzled.
Then they learned how to
read the headlines. "Very clever,"
they said to one another.

When night came, the animals
were ready once more
to put their paper to bed.
And once more Theodore
and Oscar were arguing.
"You still haven't
put my story
in the paper," said Oscar,
"and I want to know why not."
"I'm worried about
more important things, Oscar,"
said Theodore.
"Like what?" asked Oscar.
"Like the headlines,"
growled Theodore.

"We've got to make sure
that never happens again."
"But, Theodore," said Oscar,
"that's what my story is all about!

You see, the rats in our office
aren't ordinary rats, they're—"
But Theodore wasn't listening.
"I can't talk to you now, Oscar,"
said Theodore. "As you can see,
I'm a very busy man. . . .
I mean I'm a very busy cat.
No, that's not right either,"
cried Theodore.
"I'm a very busy body!"

And Theodore slammed his paw
down on his desk so hard
all of his telephones
began to ring at once.

While Theodore was trying to
pick up all of the telephones,
Gertrude hopped up to the desk.
Her feathers were pointing
every which way.
"Look at this," she squawked.
Gertrude gave Theodore
the newspaper
which had just been printed.

Gertrude kept talking and hopping
up and down on one foot.
"Look what happened to my story,"
she said. "I can't even read it."
Theodore looked at the paper.

The headline said:

RICHIPPOWNSILVERATTLE.

Theodore shot into the air

like a cat

whose tail has been stepped on.

(As a matter of fact, Gertrude *had*

been hopping on Theodore's tail.)

"It's happened again!"

yowled Theodore.

Theodore looked at the headline.
He tried to read it,
but he couldn't.
Finally, he gave the paper to Oscar.
"You read it, Oscar," said Theodore,
"I seem to have forgotten my glasses."
Oscar knew Theodore
didn't wear glasses,

but he decided
not to say anything.
Oscar looked at the headline.
Then he figured it out.

"It says:

Rich Hippo Owns Silver Rattle."

Gertrude began to squawk again.

"And so he does," she said.

"His name is Howard Hippo,

and he's such a happy hippo."

"Will you be quiet!"
roared Theodore.
"Doesn't anyone
realize what this means?
After our readers see this headline,
nobody will buy our paper.

We'll be ruined."
Then Theodore
put his hat on so hard
it came down over his ears.
"I'm going home," he shouted.
Theodore left before Oscar could
say another word about his story.

As the days went by,
the headlines
kept coming out wrong.

One day the paper said:
NOBLELKISSECRETLY
That story was
about a king
and queen
elk who
were in love.

Another day
there was a story
about a family
of geese who
went to live
in the forest.

This time the headline said:
GIGGLINGEESENJOYELLOWILLOWS.

The readers of the newspaper
liked figuring out the headlines.
It gave them something to do
while they were riding the bus.

But Theodore didn't know this.
All day long,
he paced up and down
the newspaper office,
crying, "Woe! Woe!"

No matter how hard
Oscar tried
to talk to Theodore,
Theodore wouldn't listen.
Finally, Oscar lost his temper.

He tackled Theodore
and sat on his chest.
"Theodore," said Oscar,
"you've got to listen to me.
My story is about
the mystery of the headlines."

Theodore blinked his eyes.
"Why didn't you tell me
this before?" demanded Theodore.
Oscar led Theodore
over to the printing press.

"Look underneath the printing
press, Theodore," said Oscar.
Theodore bent over
and looked underneath.

There he saw a small house
made from tiny metal letters.
And inside the house was
the Jeremy P. Rat family.

"So it was you rats all along,"
said Theodore, "stealing letters.
Well, I'll fix you!"
"Please, Theodore," said Jeremy,
"we didn't mean any harm.
We only took the letters
you used twice in a row.

Besides, we couldn't help it.

You see,

we're not *ordinary* rats.

We're *pack* rats.

That's what the *P*

in my name stands for,"

Jeremy said proudly.

"That doesn't matter," said Theodore,
and he started to
sharpen his claws.
But just then Frank came in
with a big pile of mail.

"Theodore," said Frank,
"look at all the letters.
They're from our readers.
Everybody likes our headlines."

Theodore was astonished.
He coughed
and pulled at one ear.
Then he said,
"Of course
they like our headlines.
They were my idea all along."
All of the animals
looked at one another
and groaned.
But no one said anything
because they knew
Theodore would never learn.
So Theodore agreed
to let the pack rats

live in their house
beneath the printing press.
And he also agreed to
print Oscar's story
at last.
The headline said:
EAGER RAT STEAL LETTERS.